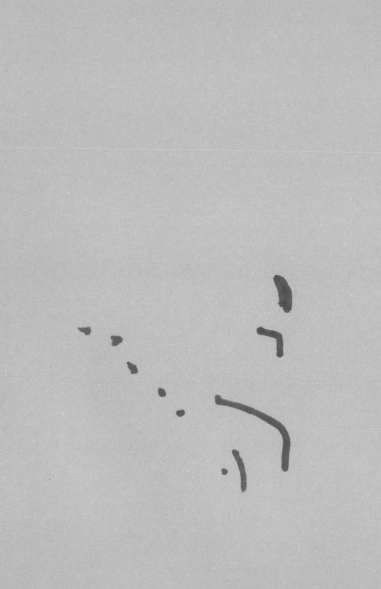

Nature Trail

Peppa and her family are going on a
nature trail. Mummy Pig asks
Daddy Pig not to forget the picnic.
"As if I would," laughs Daddy Pig.

They head off along the trail with their map.
Oh dear! Daddy Pig has left the picnic in the car.

Mummy and Daddy Pig ask Peppa if she can
see anything interesting in the forest.
"I don't see anything but boring trees," says Peppa.
Then she looks really hard and
finds some footprints on the ground.

"Let's follow the footprints and see who made them," says Mummy Pig.

"We will have to be very quiet so we don't
scare anything away. Shhhh!"

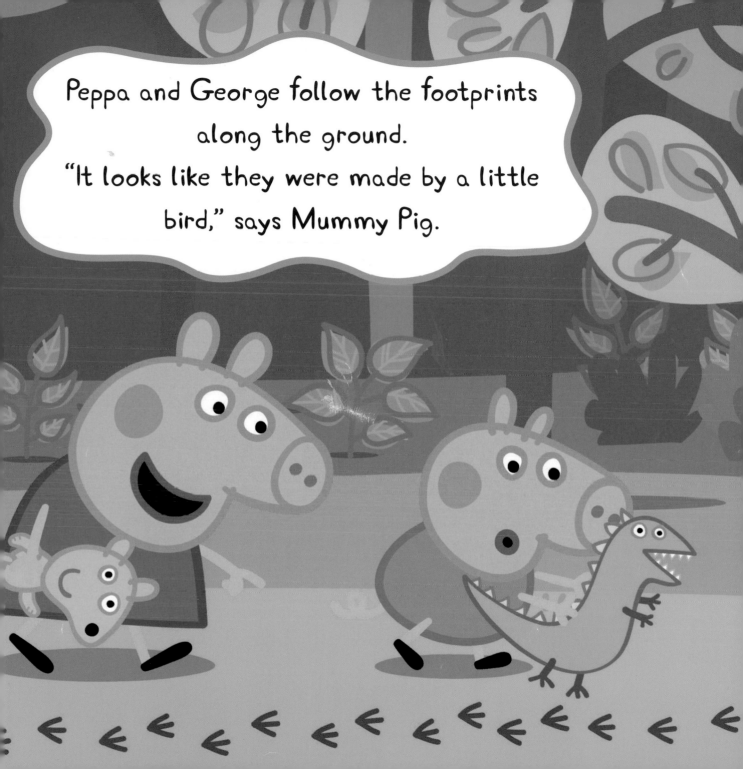

Peppa and George follow the footprints along the ground.
"It looks like they were made by a little bird," says Mummy Pig.

Soon, they come to the
end of the footprints.
"The bird has flown up into
that tree," smiles Daddy Pig.

George finds some more footprints.
They are very little. Daddy Pig says they
belong to ants collecting leaves to eat.

"My map is wrong," begins Daddy Pig. "We'll have to follow our own footprints back to the car."

Suddenly it starts to rain. It washes everyone's footprints away!
"How are we going to find the car now?" asks Mummy Pig.

Quack!

Quack!

"Ducks love picnics," says Peppa. "Mrs Duck, can you help us find our picnic please?"

The ducks lead Peppa and her
family back to their car.

"We're here! Thank you for your help, Mrs Duck," cries Peppa.

"I love picnics!" laughs Daddy Pig.
The ducks love picnics too.
Quack! Quack! So do the birds!